TEENAGE MUTANT NINJA TURTLES

nickelodeon

THE MUTANT FILES

A Random House PICTUREBACK® Book

Random House 🏠 New York

© 2014 Viacom International Inc. and Viacom Overseas Holdings C.V. All rights reserved. Published in the United States by Random House Children's Books, a division of Random House LLC, 1745 Broadway, New York, NY 10019, and in Canada by Random House of Canada Limited, Toronto, Penguin Random House Companies. Pictureback, Random House, and the Random House colophon are registered trademarks of Random House LLC. Nickelodeon, Teenage Mutant Ninja Turtles, and all related titles, logos, and characters are trademarks of Viacom International Inc. and Viacom Overseas Holdings C.V. Based on characters created by Peter Laird and Kevin Eastman.

ISBN 978-0-385-38746-0

randomhouse.com/kids

MANUFACTURED IN CHINA

10 9 8 7 6 5 4

MUTAGEN

The Kraang are brain-like invaders from another dimension. Because their home environment is becoming uninhabitable, they are trying to transform Earth's environment into one suitable for them.

Their main weapon is a powerful chemical mutagen sometimes called ooze. A little drop can mutate anything it touches. It can make normal creatures bigger and stronger, or it can combine the DNA of different species to make completely new beings.

SPLINTER

Once a normal man named Hamato Yoshi, this martial arts master was splashed by mutagen and became Splinter, a giant human/rodent hybrid. He is the teacher and patient caretaker of the Teenage Mutant Ninja Turtles. He considers the Turtles his sons.

TEENAGE MUTANT NINJA TURTLES

These four mutants used to be regular reptiles, but a run-in with the ooze transformed them into human/turtle hybrids. Splinter raised and trained them to be ninjas. They are now the Teenage Mutant Ninja Turtles.

Leonardo is the calm and serious leader. Raphael is a rough-and-tumble warrior. Donatello is a brilliant inventor who can make anything from parts he finds in the sewers. Michelangelo is a happy-go-lucky prankster. He also has a talent for naming things . . . like mutants.

DOGPOUND

Chris Bradford was an arrogant martial arts star and a student of the evil ninja master, Shredder. But a dog bite and a splash of mutagen changed him into Dogpound. He's a powerful enemy of the Turtles and remains fiercely loyal to Shredder.

FISHFACE

Xever was a low-level thug until Shredder plucked him out of prison to do his bidding. After being exposed to a mutagen bomb, he became Fishface, a mutant with a poisonous bite. A scientist named Baxter Stockman built him robot legs and a breathing device so he can continue to track down and battle the Turtles.

THE RAT KING

Dr. Victor Falco was a talented but ruthless scientist who teamed up with the Kraang. He used their mutagen to create a serum that enabled psychic powers. He tested it on himself and became a giant human/rat hybrid who can telepathically control rats. No rat mind—not even Splinter's—is safe from his powers.

MAD MONKEY

Dr. Tyler Rockwell was a brilliant scientist who was changed into a giant monkey by his devious partner, Dr. Falco. He retained much of his intelligence but developed telepathic powers. His whereabouts are unknown.

LEATHERHEAD

This powerful reptilian mutant started life as a normal pet alligator, but he was flushed down the toilet and captured by the Kraang. Before he could escape, they experimented on him, making him large, strong, and very angry.

His martial arts skills aren't as developed as the Turtles', but his incredible strength—and rage—makes him a powerful, if unpredictable, ally in the Turtles' fight against the Kraang. He really likes Michelangelo's Pizza Noodle Soup.

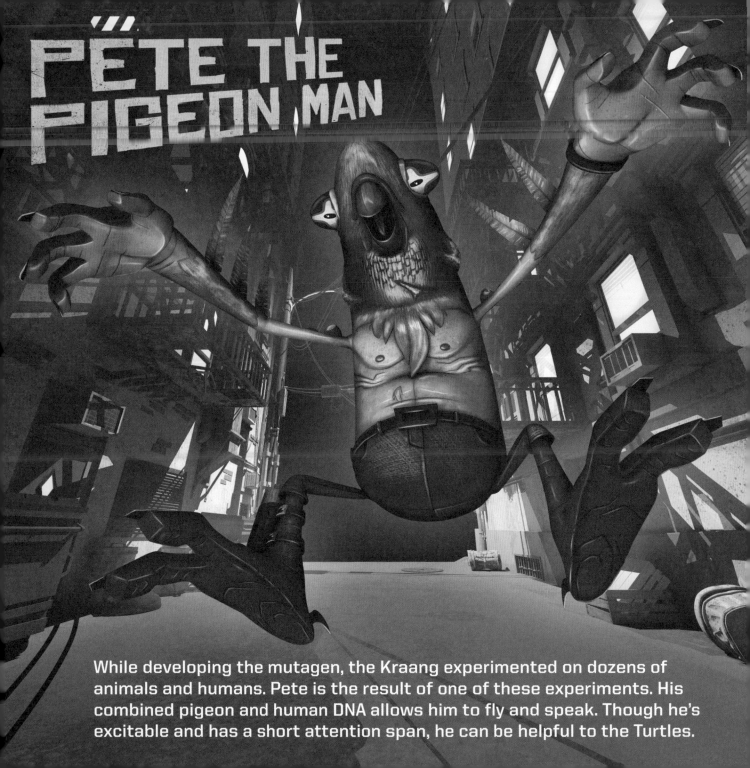

PETE THE PIGEON MAN

While developing the mutagen, the Kraang experimented on dozens of animals and humans. Pete is the result of one of these experiments. His combined pigeon and human DNA allows him to fly and speak. Though he's excitable and has a short attention span, he can be helpful to the Turtles.

NEWTRALIZER

Accidentally released from a Kraang prison by Donnie, the Newtralizer is a large reptilian creature loaded with weapons, including lasers, missiles, saw blades, and mines. Though he's an enemy of the Kraang, he doesn't like the Turtles much either.

SNAKEWEED

Snake was a common thug until he was splashed by some mutagen during a fight with the Turtles. His DNA combined with that of a plant and he began to grow—to nearly thirty feet! The Turtles destroyed him once, by freezing him, but weeds have a habit of popping up again and again.

COCKROACH TERMINATOR

When Donnie outfitted a common cockroach with surveillance gear to spy on the Kraang, it seemed like a great idea—until the bug fell into a val of mutagen. Now he's a giant mechanized monster who's gone rogue. This really bothers Raph because he has a fear of cockroaches.

SPIDER-BYTEZ

This spider/human hybrid was originally a rude New Yorker named Vic. He didn't like the Turtles, or, as he called them, Kung-Fu Frogs. During a fight with the Kraang, some ooze splattered on him. He transformed into Spider-Bytez, a mean-spirited mutant with increased strength who can spit acid and shoot super-strong webs.

SQUIRRELANOIDS

These are not your average cute and fuzzy squirrels. Mutagen has made them big, strong, and vicious. They multiply in people's stomachs, grow quickly, and *love* popcorn. Mikey's knowledge of comic-book monsters comes in handy when the Turtles are fighting these nutty nightmares.

PARASITICA

Another Kraang mutagen experiment gone bad, this enormous parasitic wasp has the power to brainwash its victims with a simple sting.

MUTAGEN MAN

When Tim, a mild-mannered ice cream vendor, first saw the Turtles in action, he knew he wanted to be a crime fighter. So he made himself a costume and became the Pulverizer. During a battle with Dogpound, he doused himself with mutagen, hoping to gain super strength. Instead, he became Mutagen Man, a strange blob with an acidic touch.

KIRBY BAT

This mutation is personal for the Turtles. Their friend April O'Neil was in danger of being hit with mutagen, but her father, Kirby, pushed her out of the way—and got splashed himself. He became Kirby Bat, a giant red-bearded, middle-aged bat.